P9-DUF-475

DISCARD

DISCARD

Handy Hank Will Fix It

by Anne Rockwell

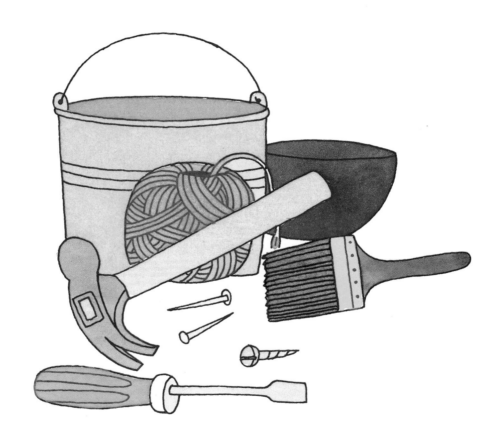

Henry Holt and Company · New York

E
R
C. 1

Copyright © 1988 by Anne Rockwell
All rights reserved, including the right to reproduce
this book or portions thereof in any form.
Published by Henry Holt and Company, Inc.,
115 West 18th Street, New York, New York 10011.
Published in Canada by Fitzhenry & Whiteside Limited,
195 Allstate Parkway, Markham, Ontario L3R 4T8.

Library of Congress Cataloging-in-Publication Data
Rockwell, Anne F.
Handy Hank will fix it / by Anne Rockwell.—1st ed.
p.   cm.
Summary: Handy Hank the repair man has a typically busy day on the
job, fixing everything from a leaky sink to a broken window, and
gets to observe other people at work as well.
ISBN 0-8050-0697-4
[1. Repairing—Fiction.   2. Occupations—Fiction.]   I. Title.
PZ7.R5943Han   1988
[E]—dc19   87-22865   CIP   AC

First Edition

Printed in Hong Kong
1   3   5   7   9   10   8   6   4   2

ISBN 0-8050-0697-4

Handy Hank knew how to fix things that were broken and did not work. Everything in Handy Hank's neat little house worked just fine. So Handy Hank fixed things for other people.

Every morning his alarm clock went off at the same time. Every morning he got up ready to start a new day of hard work, fixing things for other people.

Every morning Handy Hank made coffee in his electric percolator that went *plop, plop,* while he took a good hot shower. Every morning he shaved his whiskers with his electric razor that went *buzz, buzz.* He cooked his oatmeal over a bright blue flame on the gas stove. He took milk from his refrigerator that was always cold and poured it on the oatmeal.

As soon as Handy Hank was all dressed he set out a bowl of water for his cat, locked the door of his neat little house, and set off for work.

Handy Hank had a big green van that was filled with all sorts of tools and other things he needed for his work. On top of the van there was a bright yellow extension ladder, neatly folded. Before he drove off, Handy Hank always looked in his notebook for the list of people who needed things fixed that day.

The first name on Handy Hank's list this morning was the Jones family. They had a chimney damper that would not open. When they tried to make a cozy fire the house filled with smoke.

Handy Hank got his long yellow extension ladder from the top of his van. He extended it as far as it would go and leaned it against the house near the chimney. Then he climbed up, up, to the top of

the chimney. There, sitting on the chimney damper, was a bird's nest. Very, very carefully Handy Hank lifted the bird's nest off the damper.

He climbed down his yellow ladder and gave the bird's nest to Julie Jones. Then the chimney damper opened and closed very nicely indeed.

The next stop for Handy Hank was at the Browns' house. They had a terrible problem. The drain in the kitchen sink was all stopped up and water had sloshed all over the kitchen floor. It was an awful mess.

First Handy Hank got his rubber plunger from the green van. He pushed it up and down over the sink drain. *Glub! Glub!* went the rubber plunger, but it did not make the water go down the drain.

"I will have to fetch my plumber's snake," said Handy Hank, and he did.

Handy Hank put a bucket under the kitchen drainpipe. Then he climbed under the sink and took his wrench and removed the U-trap from the drainpipe under the sink. Water ran into the bucket. But there was nothing stuck in the U-trap.

Then Handy Hank put his plumber's snake into the drainpipe and began to turn it. *Rrrrr! Grrrr! Rrrrr!* went the plumber's snake as it twisted round and round and pushed whatever was stuck in the drainpipe out of the drain and into the sewer line that ran under the gravel in the driveway.

Then Handy Hank put the U-trap back on the drainpipe. He turned the water on very hard and it ran down the drain and through the pipe into the sewer line that was under the gravel in the driveway.

But some of the water did not run down the drain. The faucet was leaking and spraying water all over the kitchen.

"You need a new washer here," said Handy Hank. He turned off the water, unscrewed the faucet, and put in a new rubber washer. The faucet stopped leaking.

"Thank you, Handy Hank," said Mrs. Brown and Tommy as they mopped up the kitchen floor.

"You're welcome," said Handy Hank, and he got into his green van with the yellow extension ladder neatly folded on top and drove away.

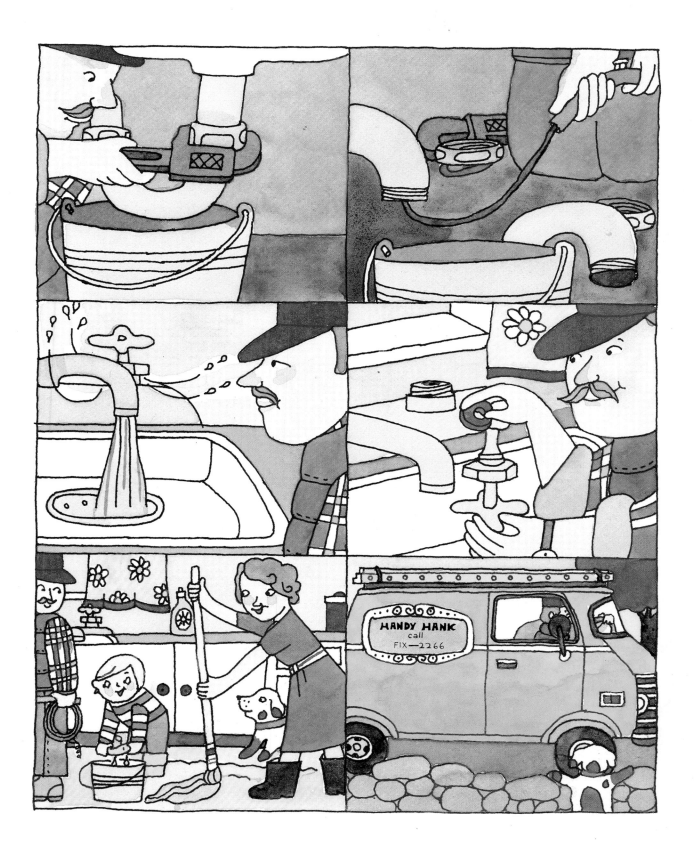

The next stop for Handy Hank was Grandpa Duffy's house. Grandpa Duffy's living room window was broken and the cold wind blew through it.

First, Handy Hank put on his thick work gloves so he would not cut himself. Then he took all the broken glass out of the window and put it in a paper bag. Then Handy Hank took his chisel and took out all the old, hardened putty from the window sash. He scraped the sash clean with a wire brush.

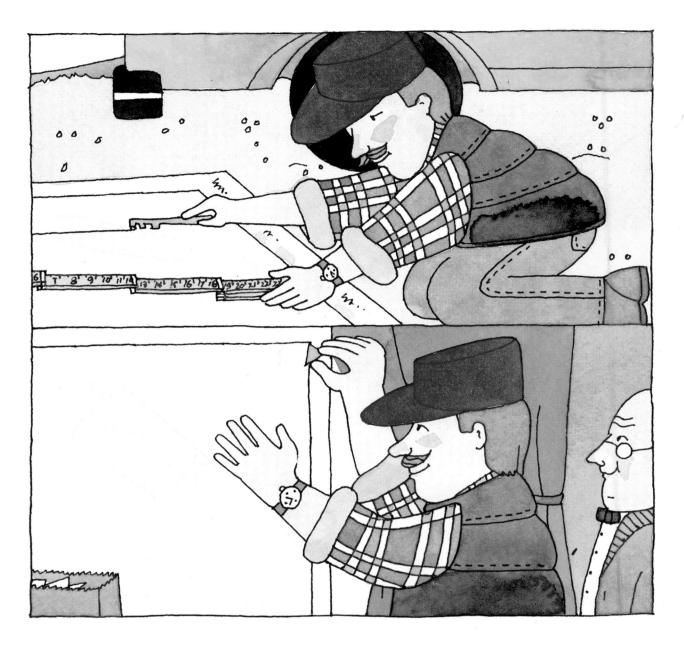

Next, Handy Hank got a piece of brand-new glass from the van. He cut the new piece of glass so it was exactly the right size for Grandpa Duffy's window.

He put the new piece of glass against the sash and put four little triangles of metal in the four corners of the sash to keep the glass in place.

Last of all, Handy Hank rolled out four pieces of white putty until

they looked like long, white worms. He pressed them all around the glass. After he had pressed them all in place he smoothed them with his putty knife.

"There you are, Grandpa Duffy. This window will keep the cold wind outside," said Handy Hank.

"Thank you," said Grandpa Duffy.

"You're welcome," said Handy Hank.

Handy Hank was hungry. "It must be lunch time," he said. He looked at Grandpa Duffy's clock. Then he looked at his watch.

"Your clock is slow," he said.

"I know," said Grandpa Duffy. "That clock is always slow, so I always miss the beginnings of my favorite TV shows."

Handy Hank opened the glass door of the clock where the long brass pendulum swung. He turned a little screw at the bottom of the pendulum, which moved the weight at the bottom of the pendulum up a little higher. Then he started the pendulum swinging again. It swung a little faster than it had before.

"Now your clock will keep perfect time," said Handy Hank.

Handy Hank had worked hard and now he was very hungry. He drove his van to Margie's Diner.

Handy Hank sat on the stool and read the menu.

"I'll have a hamburger, medium rare with onion and lettuce, and a chocolate milk shake," he said.

Margie put the hamburger on the black grill to cook. The big fan whirred and took the cooking smoke away. She put some french fries in the frying basket and lowered it into the hot oil. The french fries sizzled and turned golden brown. She put some milk in the

milk shake machine container, along with chocolate syrup, malt powder, and a scoop of ice cream. She put the container on the milk shake machine and the stick spun fast and made a frosty, frothy milk shake. Soon, Handy Hank's lunch was ready.

Handy Hank poured ketchup on the hamburger and put a napkin on his lap and ate his lunch. When he finished he paid Margie at the cash register and got in his van and went back to work.

The next house Handy Hank went to belonged to the Strasberg family. It was very old. It was so old it had been a new house when Grandpa Duffy's grandpa was a little boy. In the very old house there was a bathroom door that would not close.

Handy Hank took his hammer and screwdriver and tapped the tops of the two hinge pins until they were loose. Then he removed the hinge pins and took the door out of the jamb. Then he unscrewed the hinges from the door.

Handy Hank wedged the door into the corner and took his sharp plane and smoothed down the side of the door. Then he tried the door in the jamb and it fit just right. Handy Hank put the hinges back on the door. Then he put the door back in place and the hinge pins back in the hinge and the door closed very nicely. Handy Hank swept up all the curly wood shavings and put them in the wastebasket.

Then Handy Hank painted the side of the door so it would not get damp and warp.

"Be sure to keep the door open all night until the paint dries," said Handy Hank and went on his way.

Handy Hank looked at his list. He saw that he had one more big job to do at Doctor Bock's office.

Part of the ceiling in Doctor Bock's examining room had fallen down. Handy Hank fetched his rubber bowl and his putty trowel and a bag of plaster. He mixed dry plaster and water together in the

bowl. Then he climbed up his stepladder and spread the wet plaster over the hole.

Handy Hank had to work very fast. He did not want the plaster to set and turn hard until he had smoothed it all out.

"Thank you, Handy Hank," said Doctor Bock.

Handy Hank rubbed his shoulder. "I have worked so hard that now my shoulder is stiff and it hurts," he said. "Can you fix it, Doctor?"

Doctor Bock felt Handy Hank's stiff shoulder. He rubbed it and he moved Handy Hank's arm up and down and sideways. Then he sprayed some medicine on Handy Hank's sore shoulder and it felt much, much better.

"Thank you," said Handy Hank. "It doesn't hurt at all now."

By this time Handy Hank was very glad to get into his green van and head for his own neat little house.

Handy Hank drove down the road in his green van. The sun was setting and lights were going on in all the houses along the road. Handy Hank turned on the green van's lights as he drove along. Suddenly he saw a car stopped by the side of the road. It was a

beautiful, shiny sports car, but the man who was standing next to it looked very sad. Handy Hank pulled off the road and stopped the van and got out.

"What is the trouble?" he said.

"My car will not start," said the man. "It was fine this morning but I forgot to turn my new dashboard stereo off and now my car won't start. My mother is expecting me for dinner tonight and she lives thirty miles away."

Handy Hank said, "I can help you. Your battery is dead. I have some jumper cables in my van. I can start your car with them."

Handy Hank put on some plastic goggles. He took a pair of battery-charging cables from the green van. He opened the hoods of his van and the shiny sports car. He attached one end of each cable to a battery terminal in the green van and he attached the other ends to the battery terminals in the shiny sports car.

He turned the key in the ignition switch of his van and let the motor run and run until the van's battery had given power through the cables to the shiny sports car. Then the engine in the shiny sports car started.

"That was very kind of you," said the man. "Thank you very much."

"You're welcome," said Handy Hank. "Goodnight, and drive carefully."

"I will," said the man as he drove down the dark road in the beautiful shiny sports car.

Handy Hank drove down the dark road, too.

When Handy Hank got home to his neat little house he unlocked the door, turned on the light, and patted his cat. The furnace in the basement made a nice purring sound and so did his cat. The radiators hissed cozily. Handy Hank was glad to be home.

He washed his hands and put his dinner in the oven. He put some cat food in a dish for his cat. Then he took off his heavy work shoes and put on his slippers. While his dinner was cooking Handy Hank sat down in his most comfortable armchair and read the newspaper.

Just before dinner he turned on the answering machine by his telephone. He took out his notebook and wrote down the names of all the people who had called who needed something fixed.

After dinner Handy Hank washed and dried his dishes and put them in the cupboard. He put on his pajamas, brushed his teeth, set the alarm clock, and turned down his covers. Then Handy Hank said goodnight to his cat, climbed into bed, turned out the light,

and went to sleep.